The Blue Marlin Festival was held every spring in the village where Paulo lived. People from all over the island Santiago of Cape Verde came to see the normally quiet fishing village transform into a bustling tent city illuminated by long strands of colorful lights. There was a giant Ferris wheel brought in from the other side of the island and a band played all night on a stage that was specially built for the festival.

People ate wonderful food like marlin cakes and jam pies, and they drank tasty fruit drinks as well. The men shot cork guns at the shooting gallery for tiny cups of sherry, and the women tossed rings onto bottlenecks for beaded necklaces. The children of course ran wild, free of their parents and lost in the great crowd, the music, and the lights of the festival.

This year, young Paulo and his classmates were to perform the opening ceremony for the festival. The students rehearsed for months. They made their own costumes with shiny blue suits and fish masks in honor of the Blue Marlin. The band was to play a ballad and the students would dance like Blue Marlin swimming across the stage. Although Paulo did not like dancing very much, he was proud of the Blue Marlin mask he had made and excited about performing in the festival.

Paulo woke up before sunrise on the day of the festival and watched the workmen assemble the Ferris wheel, the food and game tents, and build the music stage. The musicians gathered for a sound check at noon, but there was a problem. Sammy Selero, the great guitarist from the island of San Vicente, had cut his hand while fishing and would not be able to play.

"What are we going to do?" the bandleader asked in a loud and worried voice. He wore a beige suit with an orange silk shirt and he was sweating. "The show cannot go on without a guitar player!"

The workmen stopped putting up the tents and the musicians stood on stage. No one seemed to know what to do.

Paulo had an idea. The boy ran off in the direction of the lighthouse.

"Joaquim!" Paulo yelled when he reached the rusted front gate of the lighthouse. "Joaquim!" he yelled again.

"Up here, Paulo!" the old man called from the catwalk at the top of the lighthouse tower, where he was washing the large windows.

Paulo sprinted up the thirteen turns of the spiral staircase and stood panting and out of breath, facing Joaquim. The boy wiped his mouth with the back of his hand and said very quickly, "The bandleader said there could be no music without a guitar player!"

"What are you talking about, my friend?" the old man asked the boy.

Paulo took a deep breath and grasped the handrail of the catwalk. Slowly this time, he said, "Sammy Salero, the guitarist from San Vicente, cut himself fishing last night and he cannot play the festival."

The old man nodded his head and continued to wash the windows. "I hope Mr. Salero recovers from his injury soon," he said.

The Ferris wheel, tents, and the blue flags of the festival were visible in the distance from where Joaquim and Paulo stood on the catwalk of the lighthouse tower.

"Would you play in his place, Joaquim?" Paulo asked.

Joaquim shook his head and rubbed the windows with a sponge and hot water. He said, "I have too much to do here at the lighthouse." The old man picked up his bucket and started back down the lighthouse stairs.

Paulo followed him. "If I help you," the boy said, "we can finish in time for tonight's music!"

"Paulo!" Joaquim replied, "I do not want to play at the festival tonight!"

"But Joaquim!" Paulo pleaded, "I made my mask and prepared for the opening ceremony!"

The old man looked at his young friend and said, "I'm sorry." Joaquim turned and walked to the front door of the lighthouse. He hesitated for a moment and then turned around, but Paulo had already gone.

When evening came the lights of the festival shone as brightly as ever—red, blue, yellow and white, strung from every tent and booth. It was beautiful. The Ferris wheel turned in the darkening sky, the men shot the cork guns for their cups of sherry and the women tossed the rings for their beaded necklaces. Couples strolled and ate marlin cakes and jam pies and enjoyed fruit drinks. Throngs of people were at the festival just like every year, but this year a big sign stood in the middle of the stage that read: MUSIC CANCELLED.

Paulo stood in front of the stage with his classmates and read the sign over and over again. The musicians' chairs were still in place, the drum kit was still set up and the bass and horns all waited on their stands for the band to arrive. But the sign remained in the middle of the stage, its two words uncompromising: MUSIC CANCELLED. The kids were very disappointed that they would not get to perform.

Then the bandleader with the orange silk shirt appeared and said, "Hey kids! Grab your marlin masks, the music is coming on after all!"

The kids cheered and rushed backstage to get their masks.

Joaquim walked by just as Paulo was putting his mask on. When the old man saw his friend, he said, "There you are, Paulo! After you left the lighthouse today, I realized that your performance was more important than cleaning the lighthouse."

Paulo smiled a big smile. "Thank you, Joaquim," he said, "thank you very much!"

When Paulo and his classmates danced across the stage like a school of Blue Marlin, the people in the crowd cheered wildly. There were hundreds and hundreds of people there to see the performance. The bandleader said later that it was the best Blue Marlin Festival ever.

Vocabulary

marlin [`mɑrlɪn] n. 馬林魚

P.2
bustling [`bʌslɪŋ] adj. 熙攘的
illuminate [ɪ`lumə‚net] v. 照亮
strand [strænd] n. 海灘
Ferris wheel [`ferɪs‚hwil] n. 摩天輪

P.4
sherry [`ʃɛrɪ] n. 雪利酒 (西班牙產的一種
烈性白葡萄酒)
bottleneck [`bɑtḷ‚nek] n. 瓶頸

P.6
opening [`opənɪŋ] adj. 開始的
ballad [`bæləd] n. 民謠，歌謠

P.8

workman [ˋwɝkmən] n. 工匠，工人

P.11

beige [beʒ] adj. 米黃色的

P.12

catwalk [ˋkæt͵wɔk] n. 狹小通道

sprint [sprɪnt] v. 衝刺；奮力而跑

spiral [ˋspaɪrəl] adj. 螺旋的

staircase [ˋstɛr͵kes] n. 樓梯

pant [pænt] v. 氣喘

P.14

handrail [ˋhænd͵rel] n. 欄杆；扶手

P.17

sponge [spʌndʒ] n. 海綿

P.18

plead [plid] v. 懇求

P.21

booth [buθ] n. (有篷的) 攤子

stroll [strol] v. 散步

throng [θrɔŋ] n. 大群

P.23

bass [bes] n. 低音樂器

stand [stænd] n. 看臺

uncompromising [ʌnˋkɑmprə͵maɪzɪŋ]

adj. 不妥協的；堅定的

P.25

grab [græb] v. 抓取

Exercises

Part One. Reading Comprehension

_____ 1. Which of the following was NOT the activity that people did in the Blue Marlin Festival?

(A) People ate marlin cakes and jam pies.

(B) The men drank fruit drinks and sherry.

(C) The children performed the closing ceremony for the festival.

(D) The women tossed rings onto bottlenecks for necklaces.

_____ 2. What was Joaquim's first response when Paulo asked him to replace the guitarist of the band?

(A) Joaquim felt honored and said yes to Paulo's request.

(B) Joaquim felt annoyed and yelled at Paulo angrily.

(C) Joaquim asked for more time to consider Paulo's suggestion.

(D) Joaquim refused Paulo's request and then walked away from him.

_____ 3. What happened to the opening ceremony of the festival at the end of the story?

(A) The children performed the opening ceremony without music.

(B) Joaquim came to play the guitar and the festival was successful.

(C) The opening ceremony was cancelled due to the lack of a guitarist.

(D) The bandleader found someone else to play the guitar and the festival was successful.

Part Two. Topics for Discussion

Answer the following questions in your own words and try to support your answers with details in the story. There are no correct answers to the questions in this section.

1. Have you ever participated in any festivals home or abroad? What did the festival celebrate? What did people do in the festival?

2. In the story, the bandleader decided to cancel the performance due to the lack of a guitarist. What would you do if you were the bandleader?

3. In the beginning, Joaquim refused Paulo's request, but he showed up and played the festival in the end. Describe Joaquim's changes in thought and attitude.

Answers

Part One. Reading Comprehension

1. (C)   2. (D)   3. (B)

 旅遊導覽

維德角共和國 (Republic of Cape Verde)

維德角共和國位於非洲西邊的大西洋，主要是由十個大小不同的島嶼組成，因為曾是天主教國家葡萄牙的殖民地，因此節慶活動深受天主教影響；而又因為國家分屬十個島嶼，節慶習俗不盡相同，但有一些共同的國定假日如下：

- 1 月 20 日：國家英雄節 (National Heroes' Day)。
- 7 月 5 日：維德角獨立日 (Independence Day)，慶祝西元 1975 年自葡萄牙獨立。
- 8 月 15 日：聖母升天日 (Assumption Day)。
- 9 月 12 日：維德角國慶日 (National Day)，紀念幫助維德角獨立的非洲獨立黨創建人 Amilcar Cabral。
- 11 月 1 日：萬聖節 (All Saints' Day)。

除了上述國定假日之外，維德角在 5 月到 8 月間還有一些特殊的節慶活動，慶祝的方式通常是在教堂舉行宗教儀式、有音樂伴奏的集會遊行，及活動後民眾一起享用專為這些節慶準備的特殊食物等。節慶的內容如下：

- 2 月到 3 月──嘉年華會 (Carnival)

  此嘉年華會是維德角共和國最大最有名的節慶，通常在位於聖地牙哥島 (Santiago) 的首都培亞 (Praia)，及位於聖文森特島 (San Vicente) 的明德盧 (Mindelo) 舉行。嘉年華會慶祝的方式以遊行為主，參與遊行的表演人員會穿上鮮豔的服裝，戴上誇張華麗的面具及頭飾，在遊行的時候跳舞，展現肢體的美感。

起源
嘉年華會起源於歐洲，是在基督教大齋期 (Lent) 前狂歡宴飲的活動。殖民時期基督教隨著強權國家到達殖民地，一些非洲殖民地國家也沿用此習俗，並在禁止販賣黑奴後，藉此慶祝自己獲得的自由權。

● 5 月到 6 月——Tabanka

Tabanka 節在聖地牙哥島 (Santiago) 舉行。這個字的原意是「小村落」，後來引申為「四海之內皆兄弟」及「互助」的意思。Tabanka 節的精神在於幽默、歡笑及慶祝的心情，因此參與者會裝扮成上流社會的王公貴族，並用充滿幽默感的詞藻和彼此交談，處處充滿著歡笑。為了要落實 Tabanka 節歡樂的精神，即使有人不幸在節日期間過世，所有參與喪禮的人在儀式結束後，都必須要忘記悲傷和死亡，並用愉悅的心情度過這個節日。

● 8 月——Baia das Gatas 音樂節 (Baia das Gatas Music Festival)

一年一度在聖文森特島 (San Vicente) 舉行的 Baia das Gatas 音樂節受到國際的矚目。每年音樂節在 8 月初舉行的時候，總會吸引來自世界各地的音樂愛好者共襄盛舉，一起享受持續三天三夜的音樂饗宴。

● Batuku

Batuku 節源於聖地牙哥島 (Santiago)，是非洲最典型的舞蹈節慶，參與者皆為女性。Batuku 分為 txabeta 及 finaçon 兩部分：txabeta 是指女性圍坐成一圈，兩膝之間塞著一捆布，藉著兩手拍打這捆布形成的節奏，來幫跳舞的人伴奏；此時舞者早已在圓圈內等候，待節奏形成，身體便隨之擺動。finaçon 是指由一歌者唱著與此團體相關的重要事件或想法的歌，並由伴奏的女性應和，形成一唱一答的合唱。

起源 ....
Tabanka 這個節日源於非洲，最初是黑奴的主人特別在這一天，讓平日遭人使喚的黑奴們有自由活動的權利而訂定；而現在奴隸制度已不復存在，Tabanka 節則流傳下來，成為大眾慶祝活動。

起源 ....
西元 1984 年，著名的搖滾音樂紀錄片烏茲塔克音樂會 (Woodstock) 首度在聖文森特島 (San Vicente) 的明德盧 (Mindelo) 放映，當時維德角共和國著名的音樂作曲家 Vasco Martins 及其朋友深受影響，同時產生了在自己國家舉辦音樂節的想法。一個月後，第一個 Baia das Gatas 音樂節就此誕生。

About the Author

Born March 15th, 1969 in Laguna Beach, Christian Beamish has always been attracted to the water. His father introduced him to the ocean at a very young age and he has been surfing for more than 25 years. In 1987, after graduating high school, Christian joined the U.S. Navy and worked in a construction battalion on many overseas

projects. His Navy travels have been a very important part of his development as a writer since he was exposed to many interesting places and people. The time he spent in Cape Verde with the Navy was the basis for the Paulo and Joaquim stories: the unique culture of the islands and the way the people there are so closely connected to the sea. Christian currently lives in San Clemente, California and has plans to build an 18-foot sailboat for the next stage of his ocean development.

Author's Note: About *The Blue Marlin Festival*

Although Joaquim and Paulo are friends, I imagined the old man being most comfortable by himself at the lighthouse. When Paulo needed Joaquim's help, it was a real test of their friendship, and I wanted to have Joaquim do something more for Paulo even though the old man has already helped the boy a lot in the past. I also imagined the Blue Marlin Festival as a very exciting event for the people of Santiago. I never actually saw a festival in Cape Verde like the one I imagine in this story, but I did come across a small carnival one night in Portugal. I was driving through the countryside from Spain and the road curved through a dark oak forest with moonlight shining down through the branches. Unexpectedly, I saw a carnival around a bend and stopped and ate some food and watched the people of the small village enjoy the festivities. The Blue Marlin Festival is make-believe, but Paulo's feelings of wanting to perform the dance he'd practiced with his classmates is true of children everywhere; even though I didn't see a carnival in Cape Verde, the influence of Portugal is quite strong in the culture, and I imagined the magical carnival I'd come across that night in the forests of Portugal being transported to the warm night of Cape Verde.

關於繪者

朱正明

1959 年次，現居台北市。

年幼好塗鴉；自高中時期即選讀美工科，業畢次年 (1979) 考取國立藝術專科學校美術科西畫組，1982 年以西畫水彩類第一名畢業。

求學時期除水彩、素描技法之外，並對漫畫、卡通之藝術表現形式頗有興趣，役畢後工作項度側重於卡通、漫畫、插畫。

1999 年驟生再學之念，並於次年考取國立師範大學美術研究所西畫創作組；2003 年取得美術碩士學位，該年申請入師大附中實習教師獲准，次年 2004 年取得教育部頒發之美術科正式教師資格證書，目前仍為自由工作者身分。

愛閱雙語叢書

(具國中以上英文閱讀能力者適讀)

祕密基地系列

Paulo, Joaquim and the Lighthouse Series

Christian Beamish　著
吳泳霈　譯
朱正明　繪
中英雙語，全套五本，附英文朗讀CD

① Crazy Joaquim　瘋子喬昆
② Paulo Joins the Fleet　第一次捕魚
③ The Apology　保羅的道歉
④ Homecoming　歸來
⑤ The Blue Marlin Festival　藍馬林魚節

一段發生在西非的島嶼上，關於友誼與成長的故事。

在西非外海小島上的海邊漁村，矗立著一座
燈塔。燈塔管理員是一個叫喬昆的獨居老
人，村民們都誤以為他是個瘋子，但八歲
的小男孩保羅卻和他成為忘年之交，並學
到許多人生哲理。本系列五個溫馨且具
啟發性的生活事件，紀錄喬昆和保羅的
友誼。清新雋永的文字，配上細緻優
美的插畫，值得您細細品味。